Sports Illustrated KIDS

REAL HEROES OF SPORTS

AGAINST ALL ODDS

BY DREW LYON

I0869275

CAPSTONE PRESS
a capstone imprint

Sports Illustrated Kids Stats & Stories are published by Capstone Press,
1710 Roe Crest Drive, North Mankato, Minnesota 56003.
www.mycapstone.com

Copyright © 2017 by Capstone Press, a Capstone imprint. All rights reserved. No part of this publication may be reproduced in whole or in part, or stored in a retrieval system, or transmitted in any form or by any means, electronic, mechanical, photocopying, recording, or otherwise, without written permission of the publisher.

Sports Illustrated Kids is a trademark of Time Inc. Used with permission.

Library of Congress Cataloging-in-Publication Data
Information is available at the Library of Congress website.
ISBN: 978-1-5157-4380-4 (hardcover)
ISBN: 978-1-5157-4441-2 (paperback)
ISBN: 978-1-5157-4458-0 (eBook pdf)

Editorial Credits
Nate LeBoutillier, editor; Terri Poburka, designer;
Eric Gohl, media specialist; Laura Manthe, production

Photo Credits
Capstone: cover (bottom left), 1; Dreamstime: Jerry Coli, 22; Getty Images: Bettmann, 6–7, Matthew Stockman, 28, Stringer/Tim DeFrisco, 13 (top right); Newscom: Cal Sport Media/Chris Szagola, 26, 27, ZUMA Press/Boris Spremo, 4–5, 8, ZUMA Press/Hennings, 18–19, ZUMA Press/Star Tribune, 29; Shutterstock: Aleksandr Sulga, cover (top right), Alain Lauga, 18 (top), Aleynikov Pavel, cover (top left), 1, Brian A. Witkin, 17, Featureflash Photo Agency, 16, KoQ Creative, cover (bottom right), Paul McKinnon, 9; Sports Illustrated: Heinz Kluetmeier, 24, 25, John Iacono, 23, John W. McDonough, 10–11, 12, 13 (left), Manny Millan, 21 (all), Richard Meek, 15 (bottom), Tony Triolo, 14, 15 (top)

Design Elements: Shutterstock

Printed in the United States 5844

Table of CONTENTS

OVERCOMING THE ODDS

Success in any sport is about beating the odds. Take baseball, for example. Even the best hitters on the planet reach base only about once every three at-bats. In other words, they fail to reach base more often than not. The key is to never give up, especially when the chips are down.

As rewarding and fun as sports are—and they sure are fun—the games can be a challenge to grasp, and even harder to master. So when athletes achieve glory in sports, they've defeated long odds.

But there's the rare breed of athlete who overcomes seemingly impossible odds. Perhaps these athletes have been discriminated against because of the color of their skin. Maybe they had to mount comebacks after suffering devastating injuries. Maybe they had to overcome disability or disease.

When doctors, coaches, and naysayers told them their dreams couldn't be reached, these real heroes of sports proved the disbelievers wrong. Their stories continue to inspire and remind us that no obstacle is too large to overcome.

ONS
HERE
MARATHON
PVV 275

Terry **FOX**:

Hero of Hope

He didn't run for fame or fortune. Terry Fox ran because he was living with cancer and wanted to help. What he did with his life raised awareness and supported the fight to find a cure.

Fox was a multi-sport athlete at Port Coquitlam High School in British Columbia, Canada. He excelled in rugby, cross-country, soccer, and, his favorite sport, basketball. At age 18, Fox received the crushing news that he had bone cancer in his right leg. The leg required amputation.

Fox didn't feel sorry for himself. He wanted to cast a positive light on the terrible news. During his stay in the hospital when his leg was removed, Fox watched children battling cancer. Fox became inspired. He vowed to run across his home country to raise money for cancer research.

On an artificial leg, Fox ran some 3,000 miles in 18 months of training. He would not be the first runner to attempt to cross Canada on foot. But no one had ever heard of a runner with a prosthetic leg attempting this feat.

Fox's mission began on April 12, 1980. For the next 142 days, Fox ran an average of a full marathon (26.2 miles) each day. After nearly five months spent running into harsh Canadian winds, Fox had reached Thunder Bay, Ontario. He was now more than halfway to his goal and had the full support of his nation.

But on September 1, 1980, Fox was admitted to the hospital after experiencing coughing spells and chest pains. Fox's doctors relayed the sad news: His cancer had spread to his lungs. He was forced to suspend his Marathon of Hope. His body simply wouldn't allow him to run any farther.

Heroic FACT

Terry Fox had hoped to raise one dollar in cancer research for every Canadian citizen. He reached his goal on Feb. 5, 1981, when the national population was 24 million and he raised $24.17 million.

Nearly nine months later, Fox died on June 28, 1981. He was only 22.

His homeland mourned his death, but Fox's legacy grew. Every year in Canada, approximately 10,000 communities participate in the Terry Fox Run. Proceeds have raised more than $650 million worldwide toward cancer research.

During the Marathon of Hope, Fox said, "I just wish people would realize that anything's possible if you try. Dreams are made possible if you try."

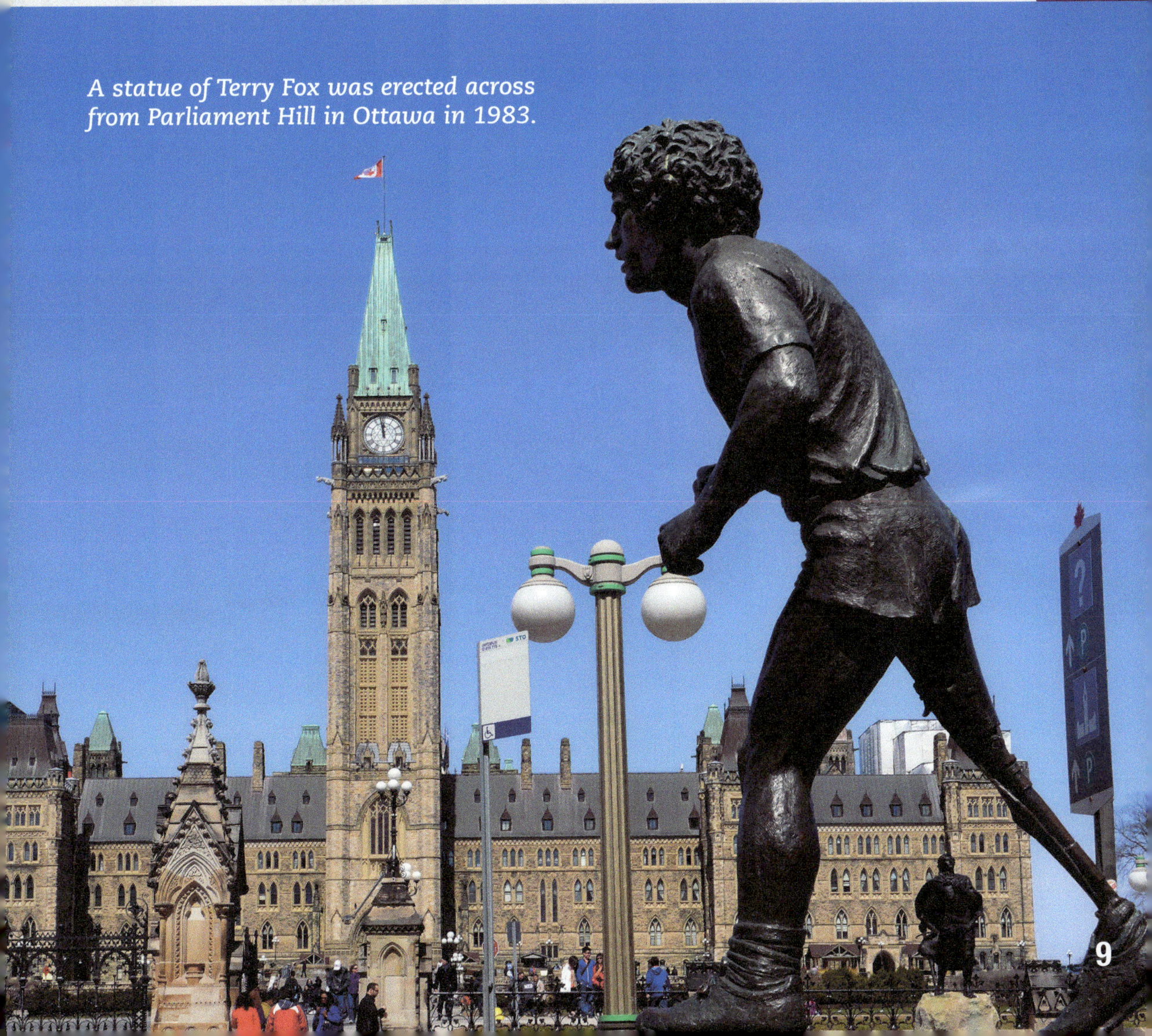

A statue of Terry Fox was erected across from Parliament Hill in Ottawa in 1983.

Stephen CURRY:

Shooting Star

Stephen Curry always wanted to play professional basketball like his father, Dell Curry. His father had starred at Virginia Tech, and Stephen wanted to play his college ball there, too. Virginia Tech, though, wasn't interested in the slim, boyish-looking 150-pounder.

Curry decided to enroll at little-known Davidson College in North Carolina. There, he grew to his full height of 6-foot-3 and hit the weight room to add bulk. Along the way, he became Davidson's all-time leading scorer.

Still, many doubters said Curry was too thin and flimsy to excel in the pro game. He was drafted seventh overall by the Golden State Warriors in the 2009 National Basketball Association (NBA) draft. One team, the Minnesota Timberwolves—having the fifth and sixth picks in the draft—passed on Curry not once, but twice.

Early in his pro career, Curry suffered numerous ankle injuries. His third season was something of a disaster. He played in only 26 of 82 regular season games for the Warriors. Those who had said Curry didn't seem durable were sounding wise.

After a second surgery to repair his ankle, Curry's game took off in the 2012–13 season. He averaged over 20 points per game for the first time in his pro career and set a brand-new record for most three-pointers made in an NBA season. He improved his game even further in 2013–14, becoming an All-Star for the first time.

In 2014–2015 Curry became a household name. He and the Warriors won the NBA's championship trophy, which capped Curry's winning the league's highest individual honor: Most Valuable Player (MVP). The next year, he was again named MVP after leading the Warriors to a record-breaking 73 wins in the regular season.

Others have been surprised at Curry's growth as a player. But Stephen Curry never doubted his own abilities. Though he plays point guard, he's been called the best shooting guard in the history of the game. Watching him toss in 30-footers from impossible angles, it's hard to disagree.

Muggsy Bogues (1) was a teammate of Dell Curry (30) for the Charlotte Hornets in 1989.

Heroic FACT

Curry may seem undersized, but he's nearly a foot taller than the smallest player in NBA history. Muggsy Bogues was 5-foot-3 and played in the NBA for 15 seasons. Bogues played with Curry's father, Dell, and was Curry's favorite player growing up.

Arthur **ASHE**: Dignified Champion

Arthur Ashe wasn't just a trailblazing athlete. He was an activist, a humanitarian, and writer who helped push a national conversation on the AIDS virus that took his life in 1993. Ashe treated people the way he wanted to be treated—with respect and kindness.

As a teenager, Ashe's lean body was perfectly suited for a tennis court. He earned a tennis scholarship to college despite being told tennis wasn't meant for people of color.

Ashe was still an amateur when he hoisted the U.S. Open trophy in 1968. In doing so, he became the first African-American male to win a major tennis championship. Subsequent victories at Wimbledon and the Australian Open only propelled his tennis career to greater heights. But what made Ashe extraordinary is the degree to which he displayed class in both victory and defeat. For this he was revered by his fans and opponents.

After retiring, Ashe learned he contracted the AIDS virus from a tainted blood transfusion during heart surgery. True to his nature, Ashe continued living with courage and integrity. In his final years, Ashe wrote an inspiring memoir, *Days of Grace*, which he finished days before his death. After his death in 1993, Ashe was honored by President Bill Clinton with the Presidential Medal of Freedom.

Heroic FACT

In 1956 Althea Gibson became the first African-American to win a tennis Grand Slam trophy when she prevailed in the French Open.

Althea Gibson

Bethany HAMILTON:

Surfing Survivor

For Bethany Hamilton, the October day in 2003 started out like any other for her in Hawaii. The 13-year-old aspiring competitive surfer was headed out that morning to ride the waves. Paddling along with her was her best friend, Alana Blanchard, and her friend's father, Holt Blanchard.

In one moment, Hamilton was lying on her surfboard with her left arm resting in the water. In the next moment, a 14-foot tiger shark attacked. The shark took a chunk out of Hamilton's board along with most of her left arm.

Hamilton lost nearly 60 percent of her blood. She survived, in part, because Holt Blanchard applied a tourniquet to Hamilton's arm with a surfboard leash.

Heroic FACT

Bethany Hamilton wrote an autobiography and went on to become a motivational speaker. Her story also became the 2011 movie, *Soul Surfer*. In the movie, Bethany performed all of her character's surfing stunts.

Her dream of becoming a professional surfer seemed lost forever. But Hamilton returned to the ocean and climbed back onto her surfboard only three weeks later. In her first surfing competition post-attack, she placed fifth.

The alternative, she later said, was scarier than risking another shark attack. "To lose your everyday life of surfing and being creative on the waves—that's scary to me," she said. "It was essential to at least try surfing again and get out there and see how it went."

The next year, Hamilton won first place at the National Scholastic Surfing Association (NSSA) competition in Australia. She won two more tournaments in 2005 along with the T&C Women's Pipeline Pro tournament in 2007 and the Surf 'n' Sea Pipeline Women's Pro in 2014.

In 2016 the 26-year-old Hamilton, by then married and a mother of one, earned third-place in the Fiji Women's Pro tournament.

"Even after losing my arm, I'm still doing everything I've hoped I could do in my future and even more," she said. "I think I'm just a reminder for young girls that, 'Hey, you can do it if you set your mind to it.'"

Kerri **STRUG**:

Vaulting to Glory

Kerri Strug was hurting, but her team needed her. It was the 1996 Olympic Games, and the 18-year-old gymnast had injured her ankle after landing awkwardly during a vault attempt.

Strug told her coach her ankle was in pain. Her coach, Bela Karolyi, said that her team needed one last effort. The United States clung to a slim lead over Russia, and the team gold medal was there for the taking if Strug could nail the vault.

Strug hobbled to the runway. She ran down the runway, springboarded off the vault, stuck the landing, acknowledged the judges, and . . . crumbled to her knees in pain. The judges awarded her a score of 9.712. The score was enough to give the U.S. the victory.

Strug was unable to walk with her teammates onto the gold medal podium, so Karolyi carried her. The injured ankle of Strug's would heal, and pain was temporary. But Kerri Strug was a gold medalist forever.

Heroic FACT

When she was only 14 years old in 1992, Strug became the youngest team member in the history of U.S. women's gymnastics.

Kerri Strugg (second from right) poses on the medal stand with fellow members of the 1996 U.S. women's gymnastics team.

Jim ABBOTT:

Striking Out the Impossible

The numbers don't lie. Only about one in every 200 high school baseball players (less than one percent) is drafted by a Major League Baseball club. Far fewer actually make it to the big leagues. The odds of getting there without the full use of one hand? Nearly impossible.

Jim Abbott didn't let the fact he was born without a right hand stop him from pursuing his dreams. He was always playing against the odds. When pitching with his left hand, Abbott placed a fielding glove on the stub of his right arm. After releasing each pitch, he put his left

Heroic FACT

While pitching for the New York Yankees in 1993, Jim Abbott threw a no-hitter.

hand into the glove. Then he fielded the ball if it came to him, pinned the glove under his right arm, and removed the ball with his left hand to throw it. Teams tried taking advantage of Abbott's disability with constant bunt attempts. But Abbott fielded as well as any other pitcher.

Abbott became a star pitcher in college, earned a spot on the 1988 U.S. Olympic team, and was drafted by the California Angels. Abbott skipped the minor leagues and had a fine rookie season, going 12-12 with two shutouts. People began to talk less about his one-handedness than his skilled pitching. In 1991 Abbott had his best season in the big leagues, winning 18 games.

The 1980 U.S. **MEN'S OLYMPIC HOCKEY TEAM:**

Shocking the World

Caption

It was a sure thing to experts: The Soviet Union was going to take gold in the 1980 Olympic hockey tournament. The question was: Who would finish second?

A team of scrappy American college players wasn't so sure about the Soviet Union. Led by an intense coach, Herb Brooks, the United States men's hockey team arrived in Lake Placid, New York, convinced they could win.

Members of the U.S. men's hockey team take the medal stand at the 1980 Olympic.

After going undefeated in five preliminary games, the U.S. reached the gold medal round and was matched against the mighty Soviets. One reporter predicted that the only way the Americans could win was "if the ice melts."

Heroic FACT

A movie about the 1980 U.S. Men's Olympic hockey team was released in 2004. It was called "Miracle" and starred Kurt Russell as coach Herb Brooks.

The ice didn't melt, but Brooks' squad shocked the world. In the semi-finals, they rallied in the third period to beat the Soviets 4-3. The victory was so unexpected it demanded a nickname.

To this day, the game is known as the "Miracle on Ice," and remains arguably the biggest upset in sports history.

But the Americans still had one more mountain to climb in Lake Placid. In the gold medal final against Finland, the United States again came from behind in the final period to win 4-2.

Anthony ROBLES: Wrestling the Doubters

During his first year of high school wrestling in Arizona, Anthony Robles weighed just 90 pounds and was considered one of the weakest wrestlers in his hometown. Robles had an excuse if he wanted to use it. He was born without his right leg and refused to wear a prosthetic leg. Plenty of people doubted that Robles could be a serious wrestler. Robles let the doubt fuel motivation.

"The same thought crosses my mind whenever someone tells me there's something I can't do," he said. "'Try stopping me.'"

Robles steadily improved and finished his final two years in high school undefeated with two state championships. Still, all of the wrestling college powerhouses ignored him. Robles decided to stay close to home, choosing Arizona State. He improved each season, and in his senior year, he finished with an undefeated record of 36-0. Because he never gave up, Robles finished his wrestling career with the referee raising his arms in a national championship victory in 2011.

Heroic FACT

Robles wrote a memoir after college and started a career as a motivation speaker. He won two ESPY Awards in 2012: The Jimmy V Award for Perseverance and Best Male Athlete with a Disability.

Melissa **STOCKWELL:**

True Blue Hero

When she was growing up in Georgia and Minnesota, Melissa Stockwell dreamed of becoming an Olympic gymnast. She decorated her bedroom in her country's colors—red, white, and blue.

Stockwell volunteered to serve in the United States Army and was deployed at the age of 24 to serve in Iraq in 2004. Just three weeks into her tour, Stockwell suffered severe injuries when a roadside bomb exploded near her. She lost her leg after 15 surgeries and embarked on a grueling rehabilitation process.

Stockwell was still interested in athletics and had taken up swimming. In 2008 she became the first Iraqi War veteran to compete in the Paralympic Games when she swam the 100- and 400-meter freestyle and the 100-meter butterfly. She has since competed in Paratriathlon and Ironman triathlons.

"Don't be afraid to go out there and try something new," she said. "Who knows, you might find a new passion."

Heroic FACT

Melissa Stockwell is the co-founder of the Dare2Tri Paratriathlon Club in Chicago. The club is devoted to helping athletes with disabilities compete in triathlons.

Glossary

accolades — expressions or marks of approval

amateur — athlete who is not being paid to play a sport

amputation — the removal of an arm or leg

durable — able to withstand force over time

no-hitter — a game in which a pitcher does not let the oppsing team get any hits

old school — committed to an established tradition

prosthetic — an artificial limb or body part

rehabilitation — therapy that helps people recover their health or ability

triathlon — a race made up of three parts, usually including swimming, bicycling, and running

underdog — a person or team not expected to win an event

Read More

Meloche, Renee Taft. *Bethany Hamilton: Riding the Waves.* Heroes for Young Readers. Edmonds, Wash.: YWAM Publishing, 2014.

Robinson, Sharon. *Jackie Robinson: American Hero.* New York: Scholastic, 2013.

Stout, Glenn. *Able to Play: Overcoming Physical Challenges.* Good Sports. Boston: Houghton Mifflin Harcourt, 2012.

Internet Links

FactHound offers a safe, fun way to find Internet sites related to this book. All of the sites on FactHound have been researched by our staff.

Here's all you do:

Visit www.facthound.com

Type in this code: 9781515743804

www.FactHound.com®

Super-cool stuff!

Check out projects, games and lots more at **www.capstonekids.com**

Index